THE ADVENTURES OF TORTI

TALES FROM WEST AFRICA

Okechukwu K. Ugorji

Africa World Press, Inc.

P.O. Box 1892
Trenton, New Jersey 08607

Africa World Press, Inc.
P.O. Box 1892
Trenton, New Jersey 08607

Copyright © 1991 Okechukwu K. Ugorji
First Printing 1991

All rights reserved. No part of this publication may be reproduced, stored in a retrieval system or transmitted in any form or by any means electronic, mechanical or otherwise without the prior written permission of the publisher.

Book design and typesetting by Malcolm Litchfield
This book is composed in New Century Schoolbook

Cover art and illustrations by Brenda Pinkston

Library of Congress Catalog Card Number: 91-70399

0-86543-222-8   *Cloth*
0-86543-223-6   *Paper*

CONTENTS

Foreword　v
Introduction　vii
Acknowledgements　xi

The Adventures of Torti

A Hole in Crow's Bag	3	Torti Goes Wrestling	36
Great Grandfather	11	Torti Goes Underground	44
The Corpse that Wasn't	16	Torti's Trial	50
Torti's Revenge	23	The Magic Drum	55
"Everyone"	29	All in the Bag	62

FOREWORD

THE ADVENTURES of Torti represents one more example of the richness of the African world-view in relationship to human development. In these stories, we are introduced to the range of human emotions, attitudes, beliefs, and concepts. Okechukwu Ugorji is at once centered in the traditions of the African people and at the same time conscious of the world around him.

As with the ancient stories told by our ancestors, these stories have a ring of power and conviction. They are elegant motifs of the ethical and moral values of Africa. In no way can these stories be seen as archaic and unimportant. In fact, every family should have a copy of this book for their children. *The Adventures of Torti* provides a great opportunity for families to rekindle the idea of recollection and retention of moral values and the ability to retell stories that have been read and studied.

Okechukwu Ugorji must be honored and respected for this strong presentation of these classic stories. Although he is sensitive and attentive to the details of narrative and character, he never forgets the principal objectives of these stories: to inspire and bring aesthetic enjoyment. His work is in the same vein as the work of the great writers of our tradition, becoming as Abu Abarry reminds us, the most ancient of all literary traditions. Ugorji captures our essence in this majestic presentation.

Molefi Kete Asante, Ph.D.
Professor and Chairperson
Department of African American Studies
Temple University

INTRODUCTION

LONG BEFORE THE ADVENT of electricity in traditional Africa, children enjoyed their evenings in the moon light or around fireplaces, listening to and telling stories, among other things. Quite often the story telling sessions brought together members of the extended family, and the light provided by the moon or the fireplace stood to assure everyone that the spirits of departed ancestors were present too. Each person had some story or stories to tell from the vast and rich bank of tales acquired from parents and elders—tales that had been passed on from generation to generation.

Those of us who had the privilege of growing up in such an environment now look back on our childhood days with enviable delight, while at the same time lamenting the changed environment for our own children. As Chinua Achebe put it, "things have fallen apart," and the present generation of youngsters are increasingly being deprived of those cultural treasures of our glorious past.

The written work invariably loses much of the flexibility and dynamism which oral tradition allows the oral artist to use in the noble effort to heighten the aesthetic experience for both himself or herself and the audience. In *The Adventures of Torti*, Okechukwu Ugorji recaptures not only the magnificence of those tales, but also the magic and essence of the oral tradition. In this admirable work, Ugorji goes beyond the translation and retelling of these beautiful tales; in the true fashion of the oral tradition, he places on the tales the imprints of his own style and perhaps part of his own personality and consciousness without altering the outcome and moral. He has done this by creating dialogue where he sees fit and giving specific names to some of the characters.

In Igbo land and perhaps in all of West Africa, not nearly as many tales were told about any other character, human or animal, as were told about the tortoise. The tales about the tortoise (or turtle, as he is popularly known in the United States of America) are not only the most familiar to people, but also the most enjoyable, especially for the children. Tale after tale documented the inexhaustible feats and maneuvers said to have been performed by the tortoise in his dealings with other members of the animal kingdom.

These tales consistently portray the tortoise as a unique and special member of the animal kingdom—he is the consummate con artist who relies on his wit to survive. In a world that is generally fast paced, his slow and deliberate walking pace appears enviably poetic; his apparent pre-disposition to be lazy is legendary; and the creator has given him an armor that proves to be both a blessing and a burden. His tricks and con games are endless and at times extremely irritating to those affected. Yet, most members of the kingdom respect his ingenuity in finding solutions to even the most intricate problems of his world of adversity. Even today, in Igbo folklore and all over Africa, the tortoise is still respected as a wise animal and a great thinker with very few peers.

The Adventures of Torti is a collection of tales about the tortoise, fondly called Mbe in Igbo land. The representative character in this book is named Torti. His adventures take him from the land to the abyss of the sea, to the friendly skies and back to Earth where all things eventually return. Ugorji successfully links tales that were otherwise not linked, in such a way that makes for a smooth and very enjoyable reading. For the children who may read this book, a note of caution: While the wit of Torti is admirable, the harm he sometimes inflicts or causes to be inflicted on others is not to be emulated.

The Adventures of Torti is refreshing and exhilarating. One derives from it the same joy and other emotions which the West African children of old who first heard these tales did. It is indeed a positive and singular contribution to not only the Igbo oral and literary tradition, but also an enrichment to African and world literary tradition.

Stephen U. Chukumba, Ph.D.
Professor, African American Studies Department
Trenton State College

ACKNOWLEDGEMENTS

I AM MOST GRATEFUL to all those, among whom Mma and Mpa were most prominent, who cared enough to enrich my childhood with beautiful stories. I also owe a debt of gratitude to the following wonderful individuals for their tremendous support and assistance: Dr. Stephen U. Chukumba, professor and author of African history, for the introduction; Dr. Molefi Kete Asante, professor, author and leading proponent of the Afrocentric theory, for the foreward; Eileen Ward, Beverly and Jacqueline Sibblies, Adaku and Osinachi Ugorji, for their support and feedback; Makini Edwards, Rene Mayle and Heather McMillan, for typesetting the various revisions of the manuscript; Dilip Kane, for computer works; and Brenda Pinkston, for the illustrations.

Okechukwu K. Ugorji

DEDICATION

To Sister Paulette Sibblies—when one can walk up to his
neighbor and pull off the powerful, seductive and often hal-
lucinogenic masks of gender, race, nationality, religion, etc.,
and still find standing in front of him a friend,
then one is truely blessed.

And to the fond memories of the late Barbara Grabowski,
Charles Walker, Al Rue, and Simon Akanwa—until we meet
again, your courage, kindness and humanity
will forever inspire me.

THE ADVENTURES OF TORTI

A HOLE IN CROW'S BAG

AS SOME TALE had it, the crow was a very well respected member of the animal kingdom. She was black in color, with the gift of the strongest pair of wings in the kingdom. She was so dark and powerful that all the other animals regarded her as the paragon of magnificence. It was wildly believed that somehow Chineke (God the Creator) had benevolently combined all the other colors of the universe and came up with the one he graciously bestowed on the crow. For this, and for so many other reasons, the crow was idolized.

Her powerful wings enabled her to fly very high and very far. Her migrations to distant lands for food and fun were legendary and well known in the kingdom. One could always find food and water at the crow's house, even when every other animal run out of those necessities.

Once upon a time, according to some tale, famine and starvation visited the animal kingdom without an invitation. It did not rain for several years, and thus the crops could not grow to replenish the farms. There was very little to eat or drink. It was one of those times when only the smart animals and the powerful ones survived.

Torti the tortoise became so hungry and thirsty one evening, that he sent one of his sons to the crow's house to fetch some water. Torti had ran out of drinking and cooking water for his family. And the crow was known for her generosity, even to Torti.

When Torti's son got to the crow's house, the magnificent one was busy roasting some fresh palm fruit, her favorite meal.

"Good evening, ma crow," Torti's son greeted.

"Same to you, my son! Why is it that I get visitors only when I am having dinner?" the crow asked in jest.

"Guess I'm lucky today," Torti's son replied.

Torti walks toward the crow's house.

"Welcome, my son! How is that mischievous father of yours these days?"

"Hungry!" replied Torti's son, "Very hungry!"

"So what else is new?"

"He sent me to borrow a bucket of water from you, ma."

The crow quickly filled little Torti's water container, and asked him if he cared for some of her roasted palm fruits. It was the custom in the kingdom for a host to offer some of his or her food to a guest if the host was eating at the time of the guest's arrival. Torti's son said he would like some. With a smile that seemed to say: "I knew you would not object," the crow gave little Torti some palm fruit and gave him some more for his father and family.

The palm fruits tasted so delicious and soft that on the way home little Torti ate all the fruits, including the share for the other members of the family. But little Torti dared not to go home to tell Torti that he had eaten the palm fruits the crow had sent him. You see, even though Torti had sent his son only to get some water, he had hoped, knowing the generosity of the crow, that his son would also come back with some food.

Torti's son decided to go back to the crow's house for some more fruits. But he had to have a good reason to go back. So he deliberately poured away the water, leaving the container empty.

"What brings you back, son?"

"The water container fell off my head, ma crow, and I lost all the water. Papa will beat the evil spirits out of me if I go home to tell him what happened," Torti's son said, crying.

"I suppose the palm fruits I gave you also fell off," the crow said rather sarcastically.

"I could not help myself, ma crow. Those fruits were really nice and delicious," Torti's son confessed. The confession and apology were good enough for the good hearted crow. She filled the water container again and gave little Torti some more fruits for his family.

"If this falls off again, I want you to keep going home, and

I hope you get some good licking," the crow warned as she sent little Torti home.

As soon as Torti tasted the fruits, he knew they were from no where around the neighborhood. The delicious fruits had to have come from one of those distant lands the crow was known to frequent, Torti concluded. So he decided to pay the crow a visit himself. Not only did he want more of the fruits but he also wanted to know where the crow found them.

"Torti! Torti! The old wise man of the kingdom!" the crow saluted Torti as she saw him at the door.

"My favorite bird in the world!" Torti returned the compliment .

"What brings you to me today?"

"I just realized how long it's been since we saw each other, Black." "Black" was Torti's preferred name for the crow, and he meant it in the most flattering sense.

"It is nice to see you again, Torti. Please join me at the fireplace."

"With pleasure," Torti walked over to the fireplace where there was still some palm fruit roasting.

"Tell me something, Black. Where do you get these fruits from?"

"Aha! That's why you came, isn't it, Torti?"

"Oh, no! I came to see you, Black. But I have to admit that those fruits were quite motivating."

The crow brought out some of the fruits from the fire and offered a few to Torti.

"Seriously, where do you get these fruits? I mean they don't come from anywhere around here, do they?" Torti inquired again.

"Of course not!" replied the crow.

"Where, then?" Torti was beginning to get frustrated.

"Way yonder, at a land across seven seas from here," the crow replied.

"You would take an old friend down there, wouldn't you, Black?"

"Not a chance!"

"Wait a minute, Black. My family is starving, and I have no way to feed them."

"That's your problem, isn't it, Torti?" The crow continued, "I didn't force you to have so many children, did I?"

"You can at least tell me where this mystery land is," Torti begged.

"Not a chance, Torti! So why don't you shut up and eat!"

Whenever a grown-up had to beg for food for his family, you knew that conditions had reached the point of desperation. As proud as Torti was, he found himself begging. And worse, to no avail. So some silence befell Torti as he thought of what to do next. That was another characteristic of Torti—he became quiet whenever he faced what seemed like a hopeless situation.

When he got ready to leave, he saw a bag hanging from a tree in the front yard of the crow's house. Turning towards the crow, Torti asked, "Are you going to this mystery land any day soon?"

"As a matter of fact, I'm going there tomorrow morning."

"And you won't take me?" Torti tried once more.

"Not a chance!"

"Okay, Black. Thanks for the hospitality anyway."

"I hope I will see you again soon, Torti."

"Maybe sooner than you think."

As Torti got up to leave he had one more question. "Do you always go to this mystery land with that bag out there?" he asked, pointing to the bag he saw hanging from the tree.

"Yes, Torti! And I am not giving it away."

"Thanks again, Black! I will see you soon," Torti said with assurance.

As he walked home Torti thought of what to do. And as usual, his mind did not fail him. He was almost always equal to any tasks. Feeding his family was no exception.

The next morning, Torti woke up before everyone in the kingdom, even before the rooster. Being careful not to wake anyone else and more importantly not to be seen, Torti went to the crow's house. Sure enough, and luckily for him, the crow's bag was still hanging from the tree in the frontyard. Torti carefully climbed into the bag and waited.

A couple of hours later, the crow woke up, washed, and ate breakfast. She was one of the very few in the kingdom who could still enjoy those morning rituals during the devastating famine. After breakfast, she pruned herself and was ready to take off in search of more palm fruits.

She picked up her bag with her beak, and off she flew, completely unaware that Torti was along for the ride. Across seven seas and seven lands the crow flew ever so magnificently. On the seventh land the rich palm tree orchard grew, which belonged to Mr. Madu. The crow gracefully perched on one of the palm trees, put down her bag on one of the fronds, and commenced plucking. Even plucking the fruits, especially as the crow did it, was art. She plucked them with her beak and carefully deposited them in her bag.

After about an hour of work, the crow felt that her bag should be full. But when she lifted the bag she discovered that it was only half full. Suspecting nothing, she continued plucking more fruits in order to fill it.

Minutes later she lifted the bag again and found to her amazement that it was still half full.

"There must be a hole in this bag," the crow said to herself. From previous experience, the bag should have been full after so many hours of work. So she lifted the bag and checked the bottom to see if there was indeed a hole in it.

There was no hole in the bag. At least not literally. But there was Torti in the bag, which was worse. As the crow plucked the fruits and deposited them in the bag, Torti was busy helping himself. He skillfully stuffed his stomach and shell with the fruits. Needless to say, he was having more fun than he had had in years. The more the crow plucked and deposited, the more Torti stashed away.

Fed up with a situation she could neither understand nor tolerate, the crow opened her bag and looked inside. Lo and

The crow discovers Torti in her bag.

behold, there was Torti feasting himself.

"I knew you were no good, Torti. But I never imagined that you would stoop so low." The crow was furious, to say the least.

"I'm sorry, Black. But I had to come with you."

"You're sorry? Not yet, but you will be shortly!" the crow promised.

Without further comments, the crow picked up her bag, with Torti still in it, and flew off. Determined to put an end to Torti's menace in the kingdom, the crow flew as high as her strong wings could lift her. She thought of dropping Torti onto one of the islands, but then it occurred to her that he might just survive the crash. She did not want that, Torti's survival, that is. So she kept flying.

"Are we going home yet?" Torti asked.

"I am, Torti. But I don't know about you."

When the crow got to the middle of the first sea (the seventh from Mr. Madu's orchard, she decided to empty the contents of her bag. And so, Torti, who could neither fly nor swim, was falling helplessly. There was no way the shameless thing could survive the fall and the sea, the crow believed.

GREAT GRANDFATHER

TORTI'S ENTRY into the sea was rather majestic. When he climbed into the crow's bag, he had not planned to go swimming, but he was now faced with making the best of what seemed like impossible circumstances.

As soon as he landed in the sea, every living thing that mattered in the aquatic world convened around him. Crocodiles, fish of all kinds, sea lions, whales, eels, snakes, and even the octopus. To Torti's surprise and perhaps relief, there was even something that closely resembled him, a fellow known as the sea turtle. While some, like the sea turtle, were filled with awe and curiosity about the stranger, some, like the shark, were ready to devour him for lunch.

"Hello, dear brothers," Torti saluted, as some of the hungry ones closed in to take a bite. Everyone stood still momentarily.

"It's me, guys! Don't you remember me?" Torti asked.

"Just who are you supposed to be, boxed stranger?" the crocodile asked.

"I am your lost great grandfather! I left the sea over a hundred years ago."

"He sure looks a little like me," the sea turtle said.

"You mean you deserted the sea?" the python corrected Torti.

"Left the sea for where?" the octopus asked.

"I travelled to a far away land inhabited by great animals," Torti replied, "and I have good news for you."

"Okay, little one," said the shark, "let's hear it. And make it quick, because I am beginning to lose patience with you."

"It has always puzzled me," Torti began, "how some of us animals are big and tall, while some of us are short and small. So I left the sea in search of something that would enable the smaller ones among us to grow bigger and taller."

"And let me guess, you found it!," said the octopus.

Torti falls into the sea.

"You bet your ugly eight arms I found it," Torti replied.

"Well, what are you waiting for?" the fish asked in chorus.

"You know, boxed stranger, for a small fellow, you have a very big mouth," the crocodile reacted.

"The name is Torti, you ugly crocodile! Great grandfather Torti. So get off that 'boxed stranger' stuff!"

"Come on, tell us the news," the fish demanded.

"I have perfected a growth experiment, but I am afraid that I have bad news for some of you," Torti added.

"That's a good one! You are the bad news, mister. Hey guys! Let's call this fellow 'bad news' from now on," roared the sea lion.

"As I was saying before I was rudely interrupted, I've only been able to perfect this experiment for the small fish."

"Who needs to grow bigger anyway?" asked the whale.

With disappointment clearly registered on their faces, the rest of the animals left the scene. The hungry ones, like the shark, concluded that Torti was not worth the trouble. But the smaller fish prepared themselves for Torti's "growth experiment."

"Well, my friends, you are about to witness an amazing wonder," said Torti, "you are about to go through a growing experience."

The experiment could only take place on land, not in the water, Torti said. So the first step was to get him out of the water, and onto the land, he told the fish. The fish carried him out of the sea and onto a beach nearby.

Once on the beach, Torti set up a fire very close to the water. On the fire, he placed a large frying pan. At the sight of the fire, the fish were thrilled, for they had never seen anything like it. Torti squeezed some oil out of the palm fruits he had stashed away while in the crow's bag, and put the oil in the frying pan. He was just as ready for the experiment to commence as the fish were eager.

He proceeded by instructing the fish to jump one after the other, into the frying pan, promising instant growth. As soon

Fish jump from the sea into Torti's frying pan.

as the first brave few jumped into the pan, the rest in the sea saw what seem like stretching motions. That was all the convincing they needed. What followed was an exodus from the sea to the frying pan. Torti just stood and watched.

When he felt that he had enough fried fish, Torti called for a break. Anxious, but willing to wait, the remaining fish took a break and looked forward to their turns.

Carefully, Torti put all the fried fish into a big raffia bag he made and tied it up. It was then that the remaining fish, still waiting for their turns, realized what had happened. But Torti was already on land, and there was just nothing the surviving fish could do to him or about their fried friends. Torti started walking home with his raffia bag full of fried fish.

From then on, the fish learned that the animal who comes to the sea with worms or "growth" formula is not necessarily a friend of the fish.

THE CORPSE THAT WASN'T

IT WAS A LONG walk home from the sea, especially at Torti's pace. The scorching sun reduced Torti to a dehydrated walking whimp. But looking forward to the nice meal he would have once he reached home kept him going. As he figured it, the bag of fish would last for several weeks, if not months. In time, all that would be worth the suffering he was enduring en route home.

However, the dehydration became so bad, and the journey so painful, that Torti decided he had to stop at someone's house for a drink of water. He had not stopped earlier simply because he did not want to have to share his fish, but he could no longer bear the thirst. The next house on the way was that of the leopard's, whose friends in the kingdom fondly called Agu.

"Agu, my friend."

"Well, Torti! What brings you this way today?"

"I was just in the area, and I thought I should pay homage to my favorite cat."

Agu was one of the strongest and quickest in the kingdom. He led a rather flamboyant lifestyle and was a very proud creature.

He let Torti in and gave him some water to drink. As they sat down to talk, Agu sensed Torti's uneasiness.

"You look a little sick and nervous, Torti. Is something the matter?"

"Oh no, Agu! I am just fine. Thanks for asking though."

"But you don't look too good, my friend. Is something bothering you?"

"I am okay! Really! So how is life these days?" Torti asked, changing the subject. Just then, Agu noticed a bag standing in the pathway that led to his house. Torti had left the bag of fish in the pathway because he was afraid the leopard would ask for some of the fish.

"What's that out there?" Agu asked.

"Oh, the bag? It's just the corpse of my dead aunt, my friend. This famine, as you know, is claiming a lot of lives. I was just on my way to bury her. I did not think it was proper for me to bring a corpse into your house."

Agu, knowing not to take anything Torti said at face value, wondered what was really in the bag standing in his pathway. Why did Torti look like a triumphant hunter rather than a mourner? And why did he not mention his dead aunt when he first arrived? These were some of the questions that Agu asked himself. So while they talked about the famine, the weather, and current events, Agu searched his head for a plan that would enable him to find out what was really in Torti's bag without Torti knowing. A few minutes later, he came up with a plan.

"Excuse me for a few minutes, my friend. I have to attend to my pregnant wife in the bedroom."

"You are a busy one, Agu. Your wife is pregnant again?"

"What can I say? Who the cap fits, let him wear it!" Agu replied.

When Agu left the room, he sent his beautiful daughter to entertain Torti. Next to food Torti loved women more than anything else. A close third in his priorities was the afternoon nap. But at that very moment, the presence of Agu's elegant daughter was all it took to keep Torti's mind off the raffia bag, and off the absence of Agu from the room.

As Torti and Agu's daughter talked, laughed, and played, Agu sneaked away from his bedroom and went to the pathway where the bag stood. His big green eyes lit up when he opened the bag and saw what was inside. He went back to his kitchen, took a big pot and returned to the raffia bag. As quickly as he could, he transferred the fish from Torti's bag to his pot. In place of the fish, Agu put little flat pieces of bricks in Torti's bag. When the bag was almost filled with bricks, he placed some of the fried fish on top of the bricks. That way if Torti

The leopard takes Torti's fish as Torti plays with
the leopard's daughter.

suspected fowl play and decided to look in the bag, he would see some fish. Then Agu tied up the bag and sneaked back to his kitchen with a pot full of Torti's hard-earned fish.

Minutes later, Agu came back to the living room to see Torti and his daughter laughing and playing.

"Keep your reptilian hands off my daughter," Agu joked.

"How is Mrs. Agu?" Torti asked.

"Just fine, Torti! She is doing just fine, thank you! I think she is due any time now."

"You are a busy one, Agu. How can you afford another child in this famine?" Torti inquired.

"As I said, who the cap fits, let him wear it," Agu replied "But I would agree with you that the famine has made life almost impossible."

"You think maybe the gods are really angry at us?"

"That's what the Chief Priest says."

Torti and Agu talked for another ten minutes or so before Torti decided that it was time for him to continue his journey home.

"You've been very kind," Torti said to Agu as he got up to leave.

"Don't mention it, Torti! Friends ought to be kind to each other."

When Torti lifted his bag, it seemed heavier than he remembered. Maybe he was just tired after a long walk, he thought. But to be sure, he opened his bag, and to his relief there were still fried fish in it, so Torti thought all were fine. He picked up his bag again and continued on his journey home.

When he got closer to home, Torti saw one of his sons playing with the other kids.

"Son!" he yelled "Run and tell your mother to make the best sauce she has ever made, for I have a treat for all of you."

"What is the treat, dad?"

"Shut up, son! Just run with the message."

Like a fox, Torti's son ran to his mother with the good news.

And in earnest, Lady Torti commenced preparing a very delicious sauce. It was indeed the best sauce she had ever made. By the time Torti got home, the sauce was ready and waiting. And so were his wife and children.

"Welcome home, my husband!"

"You're right, I am welcome, my dear. I've got enough food here for you and my beautiful children to stop bugging me for a while."

"That will be the day," said one of the children.

"What did you say, son?" Torti asked.

"He said that we can't wait for the food," Lady Torti explained.

"Just bring the sauce out, my dear, and I will show you what's in Torti's big raffia bag."

Lady Torti brought out the sauce, and sat with the children as they waited for Torti to open the bag. He opened the bag, took a piece of the fish out, dipped it in the sauce and ate.

"Man, this is food!" Torti reacted to the combined taste of the fish and the sauce. He took some more, dipped it in the sauce and ate. And then some more. Meanwhile Lady Torti and the children were salivating.

"So when are we going to join the feast? When it's all gone?" Lady Torti asked.

"Oh, relax, woman! There is enough in Torti's bag to feed a nation."

Torti took some more fish, dipped it in the sauce and ate.

"Oooooohwee," he reacted again.

Finally he said, "Get me a big basin so that I may empty this bag," Torti ordered.

One of the sons quickly brought the basin.

"Now, you will see what I meant when I said there is enough in Torti's bag."

With the aid of his son, Torti lifted the raffia bag and emptied the contents into the basin. But instead of enough fish to feed a nation, there were only enough bricks to build a house.

The Corpse that Wasn't

Torti's big bag was full of bricks, Torti realizes.

"You good-for-nothing, rotten, lazy fool! You ate all the fish, and for your wife and kids you offer bricks," Lady Torti lashed out angrily.

"I told you the dog will grow horns the day dad brings food home," one of the children reacted calmly. It was as if no one was surprised at Torti. He had pulled similar stunts before.

Torti was speechless for days. He was filled with disbelief. He stared at the bricks for days as he tried to figure out what had happened and how it did. There was no question in Torti's mind who swindled him.

"I thought I was supposed to do this kind of thing to others," he kept saying to himself.

And he could not go back to Agu. What would he tell him was missing? His aunt's corpse?

Torti always believed that there was no use complaining about spilled milk. And for him there was no such thing as an eye for an eye. No! He strongly believed in two eyes for one of his.

TORTI'S REVENGE

THE NEWS ABOUT what the leopard had done to Torti quickly spread across the kingdom like a stinking air on a windy harmattan day. Torti's reputation as the greatest con artist was at stake. The other animals were only glad that he had received a taste of his own medicine from Agu. Almost everyone wished they could boast of doing what the leopard had done to Torti.

On his part, Torti did not get any sleep for many days. He was preoccupied with what had happened to him. But Torti will be Torti! It was not long before he came up with a scheme to get even. And as always, it was a scheme worth his own signature.

About two weeks after the incident, Torti went back to Agu's house.

"Who is it?" Agu asked as he heard a knock at his door.

"Agu, my friend, it's me, Torti"

"Oh yeah! I figured you would be back soon. Well, you might as well leave, because my daughter is not in."

"That was really hilarious, Agu," Torti replied, "but I did not come for your daughter today."

"So what brings you back? Another aunt of yours died?"

"That was really funny," but Torti was not laughing. "I have a business proposal for you."

"You have a business proposal for me?" Agu laughed hard and loud.

"There are many deer running around in my backyard lately. I need help hunting them," Torti continued, ignoring Agu's annoying laughter.

The famine in the kingdom had forced everyone out in search of food, and many of the animals had become very careless about it, particulary the deer who went about looking for food even in Torti's backyard.

"Ever heard of leopards going hunting with turtles?" Agu asked.

"No, but I am not asking you to go hunting with me."

"Let me get this straight, Torti! You've never known turtles and leopards to hunt together, and you are not asking me to hunt with you."

"You've got it straight."

"So what do you want from me? Uh! Oh! I get it! You want one of my dogs."

"That's it, Agu! Just one of your dogs to help me hunt."

"And what's in it for me?"

"A whole leg of each deer I kill."

"A whole leg and a whole arm, and you've got a deal."

"I would be hunting for you then!" Torti lamented.

"Take it or leave it, Torti."

"Okay! Alright."

Agu gave Torti one of his dogs, and Torti went home. Dogs were reputed to be the best hunters in the kingdom. No other animal, not even Agu, could hunt as efficiently and effectively as dogs did.

Some dogs were free and lived on their own. Those were the most powerful and the strongest. Others not so powerful were kept by some of the stronger animals as bodyguards and domestic help. No one, except the lion, owned as many dogs as the leopard. He had twenty-five dogs altogether.

When Torti reached home. He brought out his shotgun and took Agu's dog to his backyard where the deer were. As the dog started running to catch a deer, Torti aimed his gun and shot. When the smoke cleared, there was a dead dog. Torti took the dog inside his house and cooked it.

The following day, Torti took an arm and a leg of the cooked dog to Agu. The leopard did not know what he had received. As far as he was concerned, and as it looked and tasted, it was deer meat.

"For the first time, Torti, you actually kept your part of a deal."

Torti shoots one of the leopard's dogs.

"I am a changed man, Agu. My word nowadays is my bond."

"In that case, Torti, let's do business more often."

"You just took the words right out of my mouth. Let me have another dog. I figure that with two dogs I could catch more deer."

"My pleasure, Torti! You've won my trust this time."

So Agu gave Torti another one of his dogs, and Torti thanked him. That night, Torti took the dog and his gun and went hunting again. As in the first case, Torti aimed his gun again, and when the smoke cleared, another of Agu's dogs was dead. He cooked the meat again, and this time he took two legs and two arms to Agu.

"You amaze me, Torti! I never knew that you could catch even an ant, let alone a deer."

"Some of us rely on our brains a little more, you know. And it's not by choice, believe me."

"If more dogs mean more success for you, Torti, I will give you more dogs. I mean, the more successful you are, the more meat for me."

"I could not have said it better myself."

And so the business continued. Agu gave Torti two more dogs. As much as Agu could remember, he never had such a fruitful business arrangement before. And for some reason, he never questioned Torti's tremendous hunting success. As long as Torti kept his own part of the deal, all was fine with the leopard.

It was only after Agu had given Torti his twentieth dog that he felt he should ask for his dogs back. Five weeks had come and gone since Torti borrowed the first dog.

"I wish I could let you keep the dogs longer, Torti. You have twenty of my dogs now, and I think they've been away too long," Agu said one day.

"Please don't tell me you want your dogs back."

"Sorry, Torti! But I'm afraid that I'm going to have to ask you to return them."

"I'm afraid there is a little problem," Torti said.

The leopard reaches for Torti's neck.

"What problem?"

"You can't eat your dogs and have them too!"

"Who said anything about eating dogs? I said I want my dogs back!"

"What do you think you've been eating all this time?"

"Well, deer, of course! What else?"

"Think again, Agu. You've been eating your own dogs all along."

"Okay, Torti! The joke is over. I want my dogs right now!"

"I am afraid the joke is on you, Agu. You will have to cut your belly to find your dogs, and I can't guarantee that they will be alive when you do. That's what you get for stealing Torti's fish."

"I could tear your throat right off, you ugly goblin," Agu yelled as he reached out with determination to grab Torti's throat.

Quickly, Torti went back into his shell and never ventured to come out until the leopard had left the scene. For Torti's bag of fish, Agu paid with twenty of his dogs. He learned that things are not necessarily what they taste like, and that one bad turn often begs another.

"EVERYONE"

THE FAMINE that devastated the animal kingdom came to an end. The sky opened up and rain fell to nourish the land and its inhabitants. So when the new year arrived, there was much to be thankful for and much to celebrate.

Usually the new year was celebrated with pomp and pageantry. It was a day that the animals visited relatives. Some would organize dances and plays; others just simply used the day to teach their young the complex craft of adulthood and survival.

But the year following the end of the famine, the animals decided to do something special. They accepted an invitation from the sky for a feast in celebration of the end of the famine. It was the least the sky kingdom could do after years of denying the animal kingdom rain. Ordinarily, only those animals that could fly would honor such an invitation on behalf of their nonflying kindred. But this time, according to some tale, the animals who could fly got together to aid their friends who could not fly. Torti was one of those that could not fly. From the feathers donated by the birds, Torti made for himself a couple of wings.

On the day of the flight, all the animals gathered at the kingdom square. It was an absolutely beholding sight. Everyone looked magnificent with her or his wings, artificial or real. Seizing the exciting mood of the gathering, Torti came up with an idea.

"This is a special trip for us," Torti started, "so I suggest we do something special. Let's all take different nicknames for ourselves."

It sounded like a neat idea, most of the animals agreed. So they all took different names, nicknames. They were all for the idea of impressing their hosts in the sky.

"Everyone!" said Torti after every other animal had selected a name.

"What?" the animals asked in chorus.

"No, I meant that my nickname for this trip shall be 'Everyone.'"

For lack of reasons to suspect anything, all the animals accepted Torti's new name as "Everyone." And quite happily, they all set off on their journey to the sky.

The sky lived up to its reputation. The gardens were pretty, the houses were magnificent, and the climate quite peaceful. The hosts were very kind and friendly. They welcomed their earthly guests and rolled out the red carpet in the process.

"Is it true that you guys don't get sick or go hungry up here?" Torti asked as they were being ushered in.

"That's right, earthling," one of the hosts replied.

"Man, I could stay here forever," Torti murmured to himself.

The first order of business in the sky was lunch, much to the delight of Torti. The hosts brought out the best dishes they had prepared specially for the animals. It was simply a feast for all the animals' senses.

"Welcome, everyone. We are very glad to have you with us on this New Year's Day celebration. Let's hope this is the beginning of a longlasting, friendly relationship between you and us," the Eze (Queen) of the sky said to the animals.

Then she added, "Everyone is now invited to eat with us."

As the animals were settling down to eat, Torti rose and politely but most assertively reminded them that his special name for the trip was Everyone. The Eze of the sky had indeed said, "Everyone was invited ... ," and so Torti argued that he was the only one invited to eat or at least the first.

"When I am done eating, you all can then join the feast," he said.

The claim, as annoying to the other animals as it was, was indeed legitimate. After all, they had all agreed to adopt nicknames and to respect and honor those names. It was too bad that no one else thought to take up the name "Everyone." And Torti was quite fair when he let every other animal choose a

The Eze (Queen) of the Sky welcomes the animals to the table.

name before he chose his.

Anyway, as the other animals sat and watched, Torti started eating, beginning of course with the tastiest dishes. When he was full, so full that he could hardly breathe, he told the other animals that they could eat.

The hosts were quite impressed with the apparent respect Torti commanded and the law and order the animals displayed. They had never seen anything like it before.

"You must be the chief of them all," one of the hosts commented.

"No. There are no chiefs in the kingdom," Torti said, "I am just the elder statesman."

"Well, you must be either very stately or very elderly," the Eze said.

"In fact, I am both," Torti replied.

"It's interesting that you are not the chief, yet you enjoy this much loyalty and respect," the Eze commented.

"Well, you see, respect has to be earned," Torti said. "It should be given to only those who are big enough to return it."

Then it came time to drink the fine wine that the sky hosts had prepared for the special occasion.

"Everyone is now invited to drink with us," the Eze announced.

And as the animals settled to drink the fine wine, Torti rose again and reminded them that it was only "Everyone" that was invited to drink. Here again, Torti's claim was legitimate, and the other animals had to honor it. So as the other animals sat and watched, Torti drank and drank until he could drink no more.

But the other animals began to feel that the game had gone too far. By law and by agreement, they had to honor Torti's claim, but the feathers the birds had donated to Torti to enable him to make his wings were the birds' to take back. And there was no agreement that they had to wait until they got back to earth before they could demand their feathers back. Fed up with the situation, the hawk walked up to Torti and took the feather she had contributed. She then flew off and headed back to earth. She had had enough.

One by one, the other birds took the feathers they had contributed to Torti's wings and flew off. They too were fed up. Those who could not fly got rides from the birds and the bats.

The party ended unceremoniously, with Torti stuck in the sky. To his surprise, Torti was told by the Eze that there was no room for an earthling. The hosts in the sky had invited the animals for a celebration not for permanent residency.

Torti had a serious problem—he could not fly. So he sent a message home to his wife. At first none of the animals would take the message to his wife, but the crow, still bitter about what happened at the palm tree orchard and about the fact that Torti had survived the crash into the sea, agreed to deliver the message. The message was that Lady Torti should put a mattress out in the field in front of the house so that Torti could fall onto something soft. That was the only way for Torti to return to earth—jump.

The crow did deliver a message but not the exact message. Instead of a mattress, the crow instructed Lady Torti to put together a bed of rocks and stones.

"Why would he want to fall onto a bed of stones and rocks?" Lady Torti asked.

"You know your husband. He bet the hosts in the sky that he could survive a fall onto stones and rocks."

Lady Torti knew that her husband was crazy, but she had never heard of such a stupid bet before. However, like the obedient wife she was, she gathered all the rocks and stones. When the bed of stones and rocks was ready, the crow gladly flew back to the sky and informed Torti that every preparation had been made for his landing.

After bidding farewell to his hosts, Torti jumped. Down and down, the self-styled elder statesman fell until he landed. To make a long story short, Torti's shell, which used to be smooth and even, shattered into countless fragments when he landed on the bed.

The snail and the crab put Torti's shattered shell back together.

Yes! He did survive the crash. But it took the sewing skills of the crab and the cementing ability of the snail to put Torti's shell back together. This is why today, the shell of the tortoise is rough and appears like fragments glued together.

TORTI GOES WRESTLING

ACCORDING TO TALES in West Africa, dogs were the best hunters in the animal kingdom many years ago. Some dogs, the weak ones, were owned and domesticated by man and other stronger animals. But the strong dogs lived independently and roamed the kingdom with fearless pride. And one dog in particular was the strongest of them all. His was the best sense of smell in the kingdom, and his enormous strength and speed made him an arch rival of the cats in wrestling. His wrestling and hunting prowess combined to earn him the name Dingba (Champion Wrestler).

According to some tale, Torti decided one afternoon to pay a visit to Dingba. One of Torti's habits was dropping in on friends and enemies alike. As he approached Dingba's house, Torti perceived the mouth-watering odor of smoked goat meat. He knocked, and Dingba opened the door .

"Oh, no!" Dingba reacted when he saw his uninvited guest.

"Oh, yes! Hello Dingba!"

"What are you doing at my doorsteps, Torti?"

"I was just in the neighborhood, and I . . . . "

"Don't tell me. You decided to drop in on your favorite dog."

"I couldn't have said it better myself."

"Now that we've figured out how you ended up here, would you mind telling me what you want?"

"Is that goat meat I smell or what?"

"What!" replied Dingba.

"I asked if that's goat meat I smell or what."

"And I answered you," replied Dingba.

"No, you asked what?" Torti insisted.

"No, I said what!" Dingba explained.

"What?" asked Torti.

"You've got it, Torti," Dingba replied.

"I've got what?" asked Torti.

"The answer to your earlier question!"

"What question?"

"Your question was whether you smelled goat meat or what, and my answer was what."

"That's exactly my point. You never answered the question."

"Never mind, Torti! What do you want?"

Just then, Torti looked to the fireplace and noticed a huge pile of smoked goat meat hanging down from the roof over a little fire. His heart jumped around in his rib cage like a cricket in a jar as he watched drops of oil drip down from the pile of meat into the fire, teasing the flames to near frenzy. When he finally caught his breath Torti spoke.

"Tell me something, Dingba. How and where do you get meat like this?"

"Let's get one thing straight, Torti! You are not getting one piece of that meat."

"I didn't ask for a piece of your meat. At least not yet! I just want to know where on earth one gets food like that."

"At Palm Beach Island, across the Imo River. Now, would you please leave?"

"Would you take me with you the next time you visit the island?"

Dingba burst out laughing when he heard Torti's last question. He laughed for about three minutes before he gained control of himself.

"This is not palm fruit, my friend. I mean, we don't go to Palm Beach Island to climb into ladies' handbags, if you know what I mean," Dingba said, referring to Torti's episode with the crow.

"So why do you go there?"

Dingba went into another uncontrollable fit of laughter. Then he regained control again.

"I mean we don't go there with shotguns to shoot weak dogs in the back," Dingba replied, still laughing.

"I didn't know that you had such a marvelous sense of humor. Now, are you going to take me with you next time or not?"

"As a matter of fact, I am going to enioy taking you down there, Torti. You know why?"

"No idea! Why?"

"Maybe we can get rid of you once and for all."

"Now wait a minute! What are you talking about?" Torti asked very worriedly.

Dingba then told him what usually happened at Palm Beach Island. The island was the scene of a weekly wrestling match in which Dingba frequently participated. While there Dingba wrestled with goats, sheep, deer, antelopes, cats, and gorillas, to mention just a few. The rule of the match was rather simple. If one lost, he became the property of his victorious opponent. And the victor could do whatever he wished with his conquest, including killing him for food. But if the loser had property, he could bail himself out or a friend who had property could bail him out.

Dingba assured Torti that he would be glad to take him to the island, and Torti, in his true character, agreed to go with him. He was more foolhardy than Dingba imagined.

The next day, after extensive preparation by Torti, he and Dingba crossed the Imo River and went to Palm Beach Island. Torti marveled at the apparent great shape all the participants were in. The wrestling matches started as soon as everyone was present.

Within minutes Dingba had already won his fourth match, two against goats and two against antelopes. Torti just sat down and watched the great dog at work. When Dingba won his sixth match, Torti felt it was time for him to try his luck.

Torti's first opponent was a very ill little antelope who did not want to wrestle. But Torti dragged him out to the wrestling floor. The match lasted only a few seconds. That was how long it took the little antelope to beat Torti and tie him up. Torti lay tied up on the beach for hours with saliva dripping out of his mouth.

Dingba had won his ninth match before he realized what

had happened to Torti. He laughed until his lungs ached when he saw Torti tied up. Soon, however, Dinga's amusement turned into pity. And like the nice gentleman he was, he bailed Torti out with one of his own antelopes.

Dingba went back to the wrestling floor and continued doing what he did better than almost everyone else. He won two more matches before he noticed that Torti was missing again. He looked around and found him tied up again. A goat had beaten and tied him up, ready to take him home. Dingba got to the goat in time and bailed Torti out once more. But this time, he was not amused. He was quite angry. Bailing Torti out had cost him an antelope and a goat, and he had had enough.

"Listen to me, you half-wit! Next time you are tied up, I will let them cook you for soup."

"I promise not to wrestle again."

After Dingba had made it clear that there would be no more bails, Torti, like the wise old man he was, knew not to push his luck any further.

It was the tradition at Palm Beach Island to slaughter a ram and share it among the participants at the end of each wrestling day. It was also the custom to give the tongue of the ram to the eldest animal that came to the wrestling match. Torti was the eldest animal that day, so he received the tongue as a parting gift. So Torti did not go home empty-handed after all. Dingba on the other hand had twelve goats to take home. He traded away the antelopes he had won.

On the way home, Torti offered Dingba the ram's tongue that he had received. He said it was a token of his appreciation for the times Dingba bailed him out. Knowing Torti well, Dingba refused to accept the gift. But Torti insisted that he take the gift. Finally, Dingba accepted the tongue and put it in his mouth, pretending to have swallowed it.

Moments later, as they walked home, Torti asked for his ram's tongue back. He thought Dingba had swallowed it, but Dingba was not a fool. He had expected what was coming, that

Dingba the dog finds Torti tied up.

Torti would ask for his gift back. To Torti's surprise and embarrassment, Dingba brought the ram's tongue out of his cheek where he had hidden it, and gave it back to him.

"Wait a minute, Dingba," Torti said, "Don't you know when I am joking?"

"Well, thanks anyway! I don't want your gift."

"Come on, Dingba! I didn't really want the tongue."

But Dingba refused to accept the tongue, no matter how much Torti persisted. And to get him off his case, Dingba accepted the tongue again and hid it in his mouth.

Moments later, Torti asked for his ram's tongue again. Dingba quickly brought out the tongue and gave it back to Torti. Again, Torti swore that he was only playing. And for the third time, Dingba accepted the tongue and put it back into his mouth.

Soon Dingba and Torti reached the Imo River and crossed it. When they got to the other side of the River, Torti suggested that they take a break from the long walk and drink some water. Dingba agreed. He tied the leash of his goats to the palm tree nearby and proceeded to drink. It was while they were drinking that Dingba accidently swallowed the ram's tongue. And Torti noticed. They finished drinking and got ready to continue with their journey home.

"Well, now," said Torti, "I want the tongue back, and this time I am not playing."

"But I swallowed it."

"Too bad! I want the tongue back right now!"

Dingba expected this all along. If only he had not stopped to drink, he said to himself.

"I told you I swallowed the tongue. Now what do you really want?"

"I want you to pay me back for my tongue."

"Okay! I will give you one of my goats, and we will call it even."

"One goat! Come on, Dingba! That was a very special tongue I got from the island. I would not even accept all the goats in the world in place of that tongue."

"I knew that's what you were after all along. If you want all my goats, you've got them."

Pretending to be reluctant, Torti accepted the twelve goats in place of his ram's tongue. Angry, more at himself than at Torti, Dingba gave Torti all of the goats and ran ahead of Torti towards home.

When he was out of Torti's sight, on the route home, Dingba dug a gigantic hole in the middle of the road. The hole was big enough to swallow him up when he jumped into it. He jumped in and covered himself with the red earth but left his eyes uncovered. To anyone who did not know, it appeared as if the earth had eyes.

It worked like magic. When Torti got to the spot where the eyes were, he went berserk.

"The earth has grown eyes! Everyone come and see! Mother earth has grown eyes!" Torti yelled as he ran, leaving the goats behind. "It's a miracle! It's amazing! It's incredible! It's an omen! Mother earth has grown eyes!" he kept yelling. Hearing his frantic cry, all the animals came out to see what was wrong.

"I saw it! I saw it with my two eyes. Mother earth has grown eyes."

All the animals brought out their spears and knives, and followed Torti to see for themselves what earth's eyes looked like.

Meanwhile, Dingba dug himself out of the hole, took the goats that Torti had left behind as he ran for his life and followed another route home.

When Torti and the animals got to the spot where Torti said he had seen the eyes, neither the eyes nor the goats he had left were anywhere to be found. The animals were furious. It was another of Torti's hoaxes, they concluded.

"I swear I saw two eyes right here," Torti said pointing to the ground.

But the animals were not buying the story. So they all took

turns at kicking the evil spirit out of Torti. They kicked him until his shell was cracked. Then they left him to his misery and went home.

The sun may miss certain things during certain times of the day, but mother Earth is always there and always watching, Torti learned.

TORTI GOES UNDERGROUND

AFTER RECOVERING from the beating he had received from the animals, Torti decided to play a real trick on them. One sunny afternoon, according to some tales, Torti was very bored. Staying in bed all day was no longer the fun it used to be for him. He got up slowly from bed, washed his face, and left home.

He took a walk to the market square. The market was the commercial center of the kingdom, and there were many animals, including people, buying and selling all that they could. The kingdom had just harvested its crops, so there was plenty to sell and buy. As he walked along the isles of the market square, Torti came up with an idea. From the market he walked over to the ground hog's house.

"What brings you this way, Torti?" the ground hog asked.

"Are you going to let me in or not?" Torti asked.

"I will as soon as I lock up my food storage."

"Wait a minute, Groundy! (Torti preferred to call the ground hog 'Groundy.') You don't have to lock up your storage room just because I'm here."

"Just being cautious, Torti! No offense intended."

The ground hog went back into his underground house and locked his storage room as Torti waited. Then he let Torti in.

"This is not a social visit, Groundy," Torti said as he sat down.

"I didn't think so, Torti. Since when did a paragon of beauty like me start socializing with an embodiment of ugliness like you?"

"What is this? Everyone is a comedian these days?"

"What can I do for you, Torti? Or better yet, what can you do for me?"

"I have a business proposal, you miserable underground pig."

"Cut the nonsense out. I am no kin of the pig!"

"As I said, I have a business proposal."

"Go on! I am listening."

"I need you to bore an underground route from my house to the market square."

"You mean you want an underground tunnel built for your own use?"

"Call it what you may! Are you up to it?"

"And why, may I ask, do you want a tunnel from your house to the market square?"

"How much is it going to cost me?" Torti asked, ignoring the question.

"Okay! A dozen baskets of fresh peanuts!"

"A dozen baskets! For what? Are you out of your underground mind?"

"That's just for digging the tunnel. I want another dozen baskets of peanuts if you want me to keep my mouth shut about the tunnel."

"Okay, Groundy! You drive a hard bargain. I will pay you next week, but I want that tunnel built tomorrow."

"Listen to me! I want my fee up front!"

"Slow down, Groundy! Where am I supposed to find twenty-four baskets of fresh peanuts today?"

"Well, let's wait until you can find them. But no peanuts, no tunnel!"

Torti went home and borrowed all the peanuts his wife had. It added up to only twelve baskets. The next day Torti went back to the ground hog's house. He offered the ground hog the twelve baskets of peanuts and promised to pay the balance the following day. The ground hog accepted and agreed to the deal.

As darkness fell that evening and while everyone else was busy sleeping, the ground hog commenced work on Torti's tunnel. He dug all night, from Torti's house to the market square. He was finished before the cock's crow the next day.

At noon the next day Torti took his drum into the tunnel and walked all the way to the end of it. When he stuck his head out from the mouth of the tunnel, he noticed to his satisfaction that he was right under Orieukwu, the market square. Then he settled down, put the drum in between his hindlegs, and started playing it as hard as he could. As he played the drum, he sang:

Orieukwu nesu esu	Orieukwu is about to explode!
Iya! Iya mbele, iya	Iya! Iya mbele, iya!
Orieukwu nesu esu!	Orieukwu is about to explode!
Iya! Iya mbele, iya!	Iya! Iya mbele, iya!
Anukwu gbalaga	Big animals run away!
Iya! Iya mbele, iya!	Iya! Iya mbele, iya!
Anunta gbalaga	Small animals run away
Iya! Iya! mbele, iya!	Iya! Iya mbele, iya!
Orieukwe nesu esu	Orieukwu is about to explode
Iya! Iya mbele, iya!	Iya! Iya mbele, iya!

Torti repeated the song many times as he played the drum. Orieukwu was thrown into chaos when the animals, upon hearing the song and drum beat from underground, ran for their lives. Most of them left whatever they had brought to sell and also left the things they had bought including food.

When the market square was deserted, Torti came out from the tunnel and took as much food as he could. He was only interested in food. He took the food he had gathered into his tunnel and walked home. He had enough to feed his family that week and enough to pay the ground hog the twelve baskets of peanuts he owed him.

After a week had passed by, Torti ran out of food, so he went back into his tunnel with his drum and walked to the end of it. When he stuck out his head at the end of the tunnel, he was at the market square. He settled down, placed the drum in between his legs and started playing as hard as he could. As he played the drum, he sang:

Orieuku nesu esu	Orieukwu is about to explode
Iya! Iya mbele, iya!	Iya! Iya mbele, iya!
Orieukwu nesu esu	Orieukwu is about to explode

Torti plays his drum in the tunnel.

Iya! Iya mbele, iya!   Iya! Iya mbele, iya!
Anukwu gbalaga   Big animals run away
Iya! Iya mbele, iya   Iya! Iya mbele, iya!
Anunta gbalaga!   Small animals run away!
Iya! Iya mbele, iya!   Iya! Iya mbele, iya!
Orieukwu nesu esu   Orieukwu is about to explode
Iya! Iya mbele, iya!   Iya! Iya mbele, iya!

As before, the song and the drum beat that was coming from underground terrified the animals at the market square. All the animals ran away for dear lives, leaving behind all the food that they had come to buy and sell. When Torti was sure that everyone had left the market square, he hurriedly climbed out of the tunnel and took as much food as he could carry into the tunnel. And for the next week or so he had enough to feed his family.

Meanwhile, the animals asked the Chief Priest to find out what was going on. The Chief Priest came back after consulting the oracles and said that the gods were angry. The gods were angry because the animals had not poured libation to them and had not given them enough offerings for a long time. Therefore, the Chief Priest said, the gods had come to the market square to seize the food for themselves. The animals gave the Chief Priest all the items he needed to appease the gods so that they (the gods) would leave the kingdom alone.

The monkey was one of those animals that didn't believe the Chief Priest. He believed the gods were not that foolish. The market square was a place of honor for the gods, the monkey reasoned. The gods would not disrupt anything that celebrated their glory as the market did. Moreover, he was not interested in the custom of appeasing the gods anyway, and he refused to contribute to the appeasement offerings. Instead, he decided that the next time the song and drum beat came from underground, he would stick around and find out what was really going on.

It was a dangerous mission, but the monkey was determined not only to prove the chief priest wrong (something he had longed to do all his life) but also to put an end to what he suspected was an ingenious hoax. The mission was dangerous because no one who saw the gods with his or her naked eye lived to tell about it. What if it was indeed the gods?

About two weeks later, Torti ran out of food again. So he went back into his tunnel and commenced singing the then familiar song, and the equally familiar drum beat accompanied it.

Orieukwu nesu esu	Orieukwu is about to explode
Iya! Iya mbele, iya!	Iya! Iya mbele, iya!
Orieukwu nesu esu	Orieukwu is about to explode
Iya! Iya mbele, iya!	Iya! Iya mbele, iya!
Anukwu gbalaga	Big animals run away
Iya! Iya mbele, iya!	Iya! Iya mbele, iya!
Anunta gbalaga	Small animals run away
Iya! Iya mbele, iya!	Iya! Iya mbele, iya!
Orieukwu nesu esu	Orieukwu is about to explode
Iya! Iya mbele, iya!	Iya! Iya mbele, iya!

Again, all the animals were terrified and everyone ran away for his or her dear life, everyone except the monkey. Instead of running away, the monkey climbed the tallest tree at the market square and waited.

Torti looked from his tunnel and saw no one. He came out, and as he had done in the previous occasions, collected as much food as he could and proceeded to go back to his tunnel.

"Hey, Torti! So it's you!" the monkey yelled.

Torti was speechless. He sluggishly walked back into his tunnel and went home. He did not know what to do. All he knew was that the game was over. Or was it?

TORTI'S TRIAL

THE DAY AFTER the monkey caught Torti, he went to the lion's house to tell him that he knew who had been duping the animals. But he did not want to reveal the thief's identity until the day of trial. Based on this information, the lion, in his capacity as king of the kingdom, scheduled a meeting of all the animals at the Kingdom Square. He instructed the chief judge, the elephant, to prepare for the trial of the thief, who was to be named and identified by the monkey.

The trial day was a very important day in the kingdom. Everyone was eager to find out who was responsible for the scare at the market square. A large number of the animals, however, did not believe that the monkey was serious. And the monkey bluntly refused to name the thief until the day of the trial.

When everyone was gathered, the lion rose and addressed them.

"My fellow animals, we are gathered here today because a bad omen has taken place in the kingdom. For the past four weeks someone or something has been scaring us away from the market square and stealing our foods. Like all of you, I thought it was the gods. But our brother, the monkey, says he caught the thief the other day. Yes, my friends, the thief is one of us."

There was murmuring among the animals as they heard that one of them had been doing the stealing. The elephant rose and spoke. "This court shall come to order! This is the case of the kingdom versus a yet to be named suspect. Now I call on the monkey to name and identify the defendant in this case."

As the monkey walked up to the witness stand, Torti rose and raised his hand. The elephant recognized him.

"May I address the court, your honor?"

Torti's Trial

The animals gather for the trial.

"Certainly, Torti!" the elephant replied.

"My fellow animals, today is a special day for all of us. We have all day to identify and try this thief, so why rush it. I have prepared a special song and dance for this occasion, and I would like the opportunity to show it to you."

Torti had brought a peculiar instrument with him. It was a banjo that he had made, and the animals had never seen anything like it. They all agreed that there was no need to rush the historic event. So Torti was allowed to play the strange instrument for the listening pleasure of the animals who had gathered. The monkey, still sitting on the witness seat, suspected that Torti was up to something. But he did not know what nor did anyone else. Torti might as well have his last song and dance, the monkey said to himself as he kept his mouth shut and looked on with the others. Torti then started playing and singing:

Ubor Mbekwu!	Torti's banjo
Anatanbele!	Anatanbele!
Ubor Mbekwu!	Torti's banjo
Anatanbele!	Anatanbele!
Ubor nnam nnabe, ubor oma	Torti's banjo is a beautiful banjo!
Kiribondonbo kiribo	Kiribondonbo kiribo

As the animals sang and danced to Torti's beautiful song, the scene at the kingdom square became frenzied. Everyone sang, clapped, and danced, everyone except the monkey. He could smell something rotten and evil in the song and in the tune the banjo made.

Torti played and sang for approximately an hour, and the animals danced and danced. They had all forgotten, at least for the moment, that they had come for a trial. When Torti noticed that all the animals were in a dancing frenzy, he suddenly and deliberately cut the string of the banjo. The music stopped as a result.

"What's the problem?" most of the animals yelled. Besieged,

Torti told them that one of the strings of the banjo was cut.

"Well, what can we do?" the lion asked.

"I don't know, your majesty. This was a very special string."

"Come on, Torti! There must be something we can do," the elephant said angrily.

"Okay! There is only one place you can find a suitable string."

"Where? Where?" the animals yelled.

"Any of the ligaments that run from the neck of the monkey to his tail would do," Torti answered.

And without even pausing for a moment to think, the animals took the monkey and pulled out one of his ligaments and gave it to Torti. Torti used the ligament to fix the banjo.

The animals went back to dancing as Torti started playing his banjo and singing again:

Ubor Mbekwu	Torti's banjo
Anatanbele!	Anatanbele!
Ubor Mbekwu	Torti's banjo!
Anatanbele!	Anatanbele!
Ubor nnam nnabe, ubor oma	Torti's banjo is a beautiful bango!
Kiribondonbo kiribo	Kiribondonbo kiribo

On and on the mesmerizing song and dance continued. No one but Torti realized what had happened to the monkey. Torti played for about another hour and then stopped.

"I've been playing for over two hours, friends. Let's go on with the trial while I take a break," Torti said.

"Torti is right. Let's go on with the trial," the lion said.

The elephant then addressed the animals. "I now call again on the monkey to identify the thief," he said. But at the center of the square the monkey lay dead, very dead. It was then that the rest of the animals realized what they had done. The only witness that saw the thief was dead. Torti did not kill the monkey, the other animals did it for him. He argued that all he wanted was a string to fix his banjo. He did not order anyone to kill the monkey. And even if he had asked for the monkey to be killed, the animals did not have to meet his demands.

Without a witness, there was no case. So the animals went home disappointed. There was the fear that the incidents at the market square would resume. So before they left, the animals set up a Crime Watch Committee to catch the thief. But no one ever came to know who the thief was because Torti did not repeat the game. He was not stupid. And the ground hog never told anyone that he had dug a tunnel for Torti because he would be charged with accessory. Moreover, business was business to him. He too, was not stupid.

No one who ever sees the gods after all, lives to tell about it.

THE MAGIC DRUM

AFTER THE DEATH of the monkey, Torti felt remorse for the first time in his life. He had never had a hand in the death of a fellow terrestrial creature before the incident with the monkey. He had conned other animals out of their possessions before (and he enjoyed that very much), but he had never caused the death of anyone before. And even though he didn't really lay his hands on the monkey, he was still haunted by the thought of what happened. The monkey's ghost, Torti believed, haunted him.

Torti became so disturbed that he decided to banish himself from the kingdom. So one evening, according to some tales, Torti left home and wandered into the dense rain forest. He had no destination in mind, but he knew that he wanted to get as far away from the kingdom as he could.

The moon was out that night, and it lit the jungle with authority as Torti wandered. He walked for what seemed like eternity. The more he walked, the more he wanted to walk. Suddenly, he heard a most powerful voice, which roared like an earthquake.

"Who comes there?" the voice asked.

"Who is asking?" Torti responded.

Then Torti looked and saw a gray-haired old man with a white sheet wrapped around him. What startled Torti most was that the man's feet were not touching the ground. He was sort of floating about six inches above the ground, and one could not see into or through the dark space behind him.

"Do you know where you are, my boy?"

"And I ask again, who is talking?" Torti demanded.

"I am the gatekeeper. Now who are you, my boy?"

"This is the tortoise. Friends call me Torti."

"Well, I am no friend of yours, but I would advise you to go back where you came from before you take the next step."

"The gatekeeper of what?"

"You just reached the boundary, my boy."

"What boundary?"

"The boundary of no return, that which separates the spirit from the flesh."

"You mean the boundary that separates the living from the dead?"

"Call it what you like. Just don't take another step or you will never return to your family."

It was then that Torti realized where he was. His father and other elders, including the chief priests of the kingdom, had told him about this great boundary. It was, according to what had been told, the last passage for the living on their way to the spirit world. He became nervous because only the chief priests had come that close to the spirit world and lived to tell about it.

"I will return home," he said, "but is there anything that I can take back to the living?"

"What do you want, my boy?"

"Anything will do."

The gatekeeper, aware of Torti's gift for music, reached to his right and pulled up a beautiful drum. The drum was made of gold and leather, and Torti had never seen anything like it. The gatekeeper gave the drum to Torti.

"Take this, my son, and take care of it. It will bring you plenty of food."

"No offense, sir but the living need food for the stomach and body not music for the soul. I mean, how will this drum provide food?"

"Just take it with you. You will find out. Just one caution!"

"What?"

"Never wash the drum."

Torti accepted the drum and thanked the gatekeeper. Still puzzled by the strange gift, Torti turned around and headed back home.

The gatekeeper hands Torti the magic drum.

When he reached home, he had been missing for seven days. His family was quite relieved when they saw him. They were equally puzzled by the beautiful drum he brought home with him. They did not believe him when he told them about his encounter with the gatekeeper. Even Torti himself was not sure he had not been dreaming. But he had the gold and leather drum, and that was not a dream.

The next day Torti, eager to find out what was so special about the drum, decided to play it. He was always good with instruments, and whenever he touched one, good music oozed from it. But this time something strange and beautiful happened. Food poured out from the drum and filled his house. Yes, food! Bananas, apples, oranges, rice, beans, tomatoes, bread, cassava, yams, and many other delicious foods poured out from the drum.

Torti and his family ate very well from this food. His wife and children loved him as they never had before. The days of hunger were finally over for them.

Torti came to a decision that was profoundly out of character. He decided there would be no more con games in his life. Furthermore, he decided to share his fortune with the rest of the animals. He wanted so much to make up for what happened to the monkey. It was as if his encounter with the gatekeeper had purified him.

So Torti called for a general meeting of all the animals, promising everyone a wonderful time. That was the first time that the animals had received an invitation from Torti. Filled with curiosity, they all gathered at the kingdom square. This time, no one was on trial.

To their delightful surprise, food, lots of food, oozed out of Torti's drum. No one cared where Torti got the drum. They were just happy for the feast that followed. They all ate and ate until they could not fit in any more food. For the first time in the history of the kingdom, Torti provided a feast for others, and the animals loved him for it.

For months Torti provided food for the kingdom. The

animals would have elected him king, but he was not interested in becoming royal, and the lion was happy about that.

After extensive usage, the magic drum became really dirty. The gatekeeper had warned Torti not to wash or clean the drum, and Torti remembered that. But curiosity was also one of Torti's characteristics. Moreover, he just could not tolerate the sight of the dirty drum. So he decided, against the advice of his wife, to wash the drum.

Nothing happened when Torti washed the magic drum. Nothing, until it was time to eat. He played the drum again, but the magic had gone. No food came out of the drum. The gatekeeper had warned him.

That evening, Torti wandered back into the forest in search of the gatekeeper. He walked and walked until he arrived at the boundary that separated the living from the dead. And sure enough, the gatekeeper was there. His was a permanent job. He still had the gray hair, a wrinkled face, and the white sheet wrapped around him. And as before, the gatekeeper's feet were not touching the ground.

"Who comes there?"

"Who is asking?"

"Do you know where you are, my boy?"

"This is your friend! Torti!"

"The dead have no friends, my son, only beneficiaries."

"This is Torti!"

"And what brings you back?"

"I lost the drum that you gave me."

"You lost it or you washed it?"

"I lost it, sir."

And for lying, the gatekeeper reached to his left and pulled up another drum. The drum looked just like the first one. He gave it to Torti and warned him again not to wash it. Torti accepted the drum, thanked the gatekeeper, and went home. He rejoiced all the way home.

When it was time to eat the next day, Torti summoned his family to the dining room and started playing his new drum.

And as with the first drum, something strange happened. But instead of food, bees and wasps poured out of the drum as if they had been waiting for years to be set free. They filled Torti's house and stung him and his family so badly that their faces swelled beyond recognition. They were sick for weeks.

In his new spirit of sharing, Torti called all the animals together again, promising them a wonderful time. As had been the case for the past months, all the animals gathered at the kingdom square hoping to eat and drink. But as Torti played his drum, the animals were mercilessly mugged by bees and wasps. The feast had taken a different turn. While the animals were being stung, Torti withdrew into his shell. The party ended almost as soon as it had started.

The animals run from the bees and wasps.

ALL IN THE BAG

AFTER THE INCIDENT with the bees and the wasps, Torti decided he had had enough of the con artist life. He had played all the tricks in the books and many that were not in the book. As far as he was concerned, he was the smartest and wisest animal in the kingdom, and he wanted not only to be remembered by that but also wanted to preserve his wisdom and knowledge.

So he decided to put his tricks and wisdom in one big bag for preservation. But more importantly, he wanted no one else to know what he knew. He wanted a monopoly on wisdom and knowledge. So when he had put all the knowledge and wisdom in the big bag, he tied the bag up and headed for the tallest tree in the kingdom.

When Torti got to the tallest tree in the kingdom, his plan was to climb to the top of it and leave the bag of wisdom there, out of the reach of the other animals. He attached a string to the bag and tied the other end of the string to his neck, with the bag hanging in front of him and resting on his stomach.

Then Torti proceeded to climb the tallest tree. But when he tried to climb, he could not. The big bag of wisdom hanging from his neck and resting on his stomach was in the way. He persisted in his attempt to climb the tree and failed each time. He could not get a tight enough grip on the tree because the bag was in the way, and he did not know just how to solve the problem.

Luckily, the rabbit walked by and saw Torti sweating and panting around the tree.

"What's the problem, Torti?"

"Man, I've been trying to climb this tree without success for the past three hours. I have to get to the top of the tree."

"Let me see you try it once again."

All in the Bag

Torti reaches the top of the tree.

Torti attempted the climb, and once again, he fell from the tree.

"Have you tried switching the bag around so that it hangs behind you and rests on your back?" the rabbit asked.

Torti said, "no." He saw no point in the suggestion but went ahead and gave it a try anyway. He turned the bag around so that it hung behind him and rested on his back. Then he attempted the climb again, and this time he climbed with ease. The bag was no longer in the way, and the climb to the top of the tree was simple and smooth. He thanked the rabbit, who then continued on his way to wherever he was going.

When Torti got to the top of the tree, he untied the big bag of wisdom from his neck and hung it on one of the branches.

"I now have a monopoly on wisdom and knowledge! I am indeed the wisest and smartest of them all," Torti said as he celebrated and rejoiced over his latest accomplishment.

It was only after he started coming down from the tallest tree that a terribly disappointing thought occurred to him. He realized, very much to his agony, that it was the rabbit who taught him how to climb to the top of the tree with the big bag of wisdom.

"That miserable thing with big funny ears knew something I didn't," he lamented to himself. It was a devastating blow to one of the biggest egos in the kingdom. Sadly, but inevitably, he came to the conclusion that he did not have a monopoly on wisdom and knowledge after all.

Angry and disappointed, Torti climbed back up. He grabbed the big bag of wisdom, the bag that was supposed to hold all the wisdom in the world, and threw it down furiously. He wanted to start all over again. He quietly climbed down from the tree, and off he went, on a mission to gather more knowledge and wisdom. Off he went—on a journey for more adventures.

Disappointed, Torti walks off for more adventures.

the wisdom in the world, and threw it down furiously. He wanted to start all over again. He quietly climbed down from the tree, and off he went, on a mission to gather more knowledge and wisdom. Off he went—on a journey for more adventures.